Life is Not a Trifling Affair

A Collection of Short Stories

by

Elizabeth Ducie and Sharon Cook

Chudleigh Phoenix Publications

A Chudleigh Phoenix Publications book

ISBN: 978-0-9569508-0-2

Printed by Hedgerow Print, Crediton, Devon EX17 1ES

Chudleigh Phoenix Publications
A Division of
The Chudleigh Phoenix Community Magazine

Contents

About the authors

Elizabeth Ducie moved with her husband to the south-west for its rich, green scenery after many years in the arid south-east. She forgot to ask why the countryside was so green – but has now invested in a pair of wellies, so is very happy. Elizabeth lives a secret life as an international jet-setter. When she grows up, she wants to be a best-selling novelist and live in a cottage with roses around the door. To date, she's got as far as the roses.

Sharon Cook skidded to a halt in Devon just three years ago, with two young children in tow. From their seventeenth-century cottage, she is fulfilling a dream of the five-year-old she once was and, when not avoiding housework, she writes. Building on 20 years experience as a journalist and food writer, Sharon remains utterly fascinated by people. Making quilts and chutney keeps her sane… sometimes.

***

This book is dedicated to Harrison and Poppy, who are wonderful – even when they aren't. And to Michael and Alex – enough said

For more information about the authors or about Chudleigh Phoenix Publications, visit our website at www.chudleighphoenix.co.uk

Cut and Paste
Sharon Cook

The box contained scraps. Lots and lots of scraps. Some large, some quite miniscule but all brightly coloured and all with some kind of pattern.

"What on earth...?" puzzled Anthea.

"Must have come from a quilters house," lobbed in Marcia, "My nan used to quilt – well, back in the days when it was out of necessity, not for pure pleasure."

"Quilt? Quilt what?" responded Anthea, even more bemused.

"Fabric, silly!" laughed Marcia. "My nan used to make patchwork quilts. All the beds ended up with one, and most welcome they were too. Her house was always so damn cold, even in the summer".

"But why would someone bring in a box of fabric scraps?" persisted Anthea. "Surely no one would want to buy them?"

Marcia stood behind the counter of the rather shabby little charity shop, and smiled.

Anthea hated it when the older woman did that. It made her feel rather uncomfortable, as if Marcia knew something she didn't. As if she was in on some sort of cosmic joke which only Anthea never quite got.

"OK. This is the deal," said a short, somewhat rotund Marcia, in an unmistakably superior fashion. "You have them, and make a quilt."

"Erm – me? Make a quilt?" responded Anthea, somewhat grumpily. "I don't think so. I wouldn't know where to start. It's just not my thing. I, well, I just don't really..."

Just as Anthea realised Marcia was so busy rummaging through the pile of stuff that someone had just donated she wasn't listening, it was too late.

"Ah, here we are. Don't normally get one without the other," soothed Marcia, triumphantly holding aloft a whole bunch of magazines. Quilting magazines.

"Right. Take the box of scraps – and the magazines. And get sewing. And don't tell me you haven't got a sewing machine, because I know you made the curtains in your lounge," laughed Marcia.

"But I…" and before Anthea could blurt out "hate sewing" Marcia pulled out her trump card.

"It's a Bank Holiday weekend. And you did say you had nothing planned. Trust me, you'll be hooked. I'll come round and help if you want," added Marcia, somewhat sneakily. She knew Anthea was averse to having people visit her home at short notice, preferring to spend at least half a day cleaning and tidying. She was one of those: 'Oh, the house is such a mess' martyrs, who needed people to think she lived in a permanent state of perfection.

In fact the more Anthea protested, the more Marcia realised she had found another perfect solution. The tall, willowy and undeniably sleek Anthea needed a bit of unpredictability in her life. Everything was far too ordered. A bit of random fabric, some creativity, a sense of achievement, purpose. It was perfect!

Having worked in the charity shop for more than 20 years, Marcia knew people often needed to be matched up with the unwanted detritus of others. All sorts of magic could follow.

It wasn't just about raising money for the children's hospice. It was as much about helping the many people who wandered through the doors of the badly painted shop.

And that meant the volunteers who staffed it as much as the collectors, the financially challenged, the green brigade and the penny-astutes who were always looking for a bargain.

Marcia knew all about being careful with money. She'd lived most of her almost seventy years (though she didn't look a day over sixty) with very little money. Having single-handedly raised three children after being widowed at just 27, Marcia was the ultimate penny pincher. She knew a thing or two about being lonely – and young lives cut short.

She understood working for such a charity often brought in women who had been touched by the loss of a child – very often grandmothers.

Anthea was a case in point.

She had lost her only grandson to cancer when he was just five, and now she wanted to 'do her bit' for other families. It was all so terribly sad, so horribly unfair, the death of a child.

Yet working in the charity shop really did help.

It took the edge off that feeling of helplessness which so often accompanied serious illness. It filled time. And it was often quite a laugh.

It was quite staggering just what people donated to charity shops. Clothes and crockery, old vases, forks, unwanted bath salts (unopened!), garden ornaments, old pictures, valuable antiques - once, even a diamond ring –

garden tools, mini greenhouses, cat bowls, vintage china and handbags. The list was endlessly surprising.

Marcia did, however, have to warn all volunteers to check pockets carefully. Watch for sharp items, five pound notes (!) and not to be surprised if they found the odd rather undesirable unmentionable. Quite unbelievable were people, knew Marcia.

Also, unbelievably generous. Which is how the children's hospice up the road was able to help so many people.

But back to the job in hand.

"There are a few cotton shirts out the back that have been hanging around for ages," Marcia told Anthea. "Take them with you. You can cut them up too. You need to fiddle about. My advice – wash everything first then, as you iron it all, you'll get to know what you've got to work with."

"I think," said Anthea, trying not to laugh, "that you are a bossy old woman."

"And it's taken you this long to work that out?" retorted Marcia, a large grin spreading across her lipsticked lips.

"Do I have a choice about this fabric, then?" pondered Anthea, out loud.

"Well, here's the deal," repeated Marcia. See what happens. If you enjoy it then maybe you can make a quilt and we'll raffle it in the shop. If you really don't like it, then I'm sure some fabriholic will wander into the shop and snap up whatever you don't use."

By the time Anthea had returned home with the box of fabric, old shirts and magazines she was just ever so slightly cross with herself.

Why on earth had she agreed to this? It would all just cause a mess. And besides, Anthea really didn't believe she was at all creative. In fact, since the death last year of her beloved grandson Thomas, Anthea's life had seemed quite devoid of so much.

A cold-hearted daughter-in-law who was still grieving. Her only son an emotional recluse at the best of times. The now childless couple who lived too far away for casual visits, even if she had been welcome. And now, another Bank Holiday to wade through. Three days of solitude. Another trip out to a stately home, perhaps? A new recipe would mean driving to the supermarket – maybe she could pick up a new book, or a new skirt?

A familiar feeling of emptiness swept over Anthea. Both options meant coming back to an empty house. There was nothing left in her home to sort, to re-organise, to clear, to revamp. Even the garden was fully pruned and primped, each shrub a delight, every pot fully deadheaded. Not a weed in sight.

While she had some lovely friends, Anthea lived on an island of singledom. With no immediate family to hand, and no 'significant other', she found herself an unwitting reject at most social gatherings. Glamorous widows with the added complication of a tragic grandchild's death – well, quite frankly, she was a social complication too far in such a well-ordered village.

Reluctantly, Anthea tipped the box upside down and, despite her reservations, she soon found herself making little piles of fabric, matching like colours,

5

picking out a couple of larger pieces, putting aside a beautiful green and blue strip that she found particularly inspiring.

On went the washing machine. Out came the iron. Before Anthea realised she was actually quite hungry she'd been fiddling with fabric for almost four hours.

By the time of her next shift in the charity shop the following week Anthea had, to her utter surprise and delight, made a lap quilt.

As soon as Marcia clapped eyes on it she was stunned at just how Anthea had taken to such an inexplicable form of alchemy.

In fact, Anthea was so taken with her new hobby that within six months of taking home the box she had turned her spare bedroom into a sewing room and had started collecting fabric from wherever she could find it.

Quilt shops, jumble sales, other charity shops, table top events, craft fayres, the village fete – all offered fabric opportunities.

Marcia became very smug, even encouraging Anthea to start making quilts for the hospice itself.

***

By the time Marcia was diagnosed with advanced bowel cancer, Anthea was involved with two quilting groups, and was frequently asked to exhibit some of her more "arty" pieces.

As a thank you to Marcia for her encouragement, Anthea presented her mentor with a beautifully hand quilted, log cabin bedspread in browns and oranges on her last day at the charity shop.

"Oh my dear," said a weary Marcia, "I am touched and delighted. It is utterly beautiful. Now please, can you take me home?"

As Anthea walked Marcia up her driveway the older woman invited her in for a sherry. "It's been a busy day. And I have something to show you…"

Taking Anthea by the hand, Marcia took her on a tour of her modest and chaotic bungalow.

Every single room was adorned with quilts – on beds, on sofas, on walls, as pillows, pot holders, bags, table runners. Piles of fabric graced every nook and cranny.

"It was you, wasn't it?" grinned Anthea. "You brought the fabric and the magazines into the charity shop – you set me up!"

Marcia grinned back. "It's all part of the service!"

***

Marcia was buried two weeks later and, at her behest, the coffin was draped with Anthea's log cabin quilt. The new vicar was so enchanted by the design he invited Anthea round to the rectory to discuss a commission – over sherry.

The Honeybee Mafia
Elizabeth Ducie

Melanie's scream ripped through the early morning hubbub at Beehives, just as the residents were settling down to breakfast. Freda Jones jumped in her seat, dropped her spoon back into her porridge and exclaimed loudly as the thick liquid flew up.

"Now look what's happened! I've got porridge on my best cardigan" she wailed, scrubbing at the embroidered roses with her napkin. She always wore this cardigan on Wednesdays, since one of the window cleaners told her it matched the blue of her eyes.

All the others stopped what they were doing to see who was causing the commotion. Even Gilbert Hodges sensed there was something amiss, and he wasn't wearing his hearing aid. He never did wear it before noon, saying he enjoyed the peace and tranquillity.

Jennie and Flora came out of the kitchen, expecting to see one of the residents collapsed (or worse). Jennie was running, with a look of concern on her face, like a mother lion hearing a distressed cub.

"Come on Flora, get a move on. I may need your help" she called, looking over her shoulder. Her auburn hair swung around her face and her many bangles clicked like castanets.

"I'm doing the best I can, Jennie" grumbled Flora. "You know I have to watch my breathing problems. And my feet are really playing me up this week."

Flora would never be a good advertisement for the low-cholesterol spread that shared her name. She always ambled at the same pace, whether she was bringing out the tea trolley, answering the door to 'that nice young doctor from the local practice' or coming to tell cook that she 'could smell burning from the kitchen and how long did she say to set the timer for?'

Melanie Howells was a longstanding and popular member of the community, recently passing her seventy eighth birthday. She was a small, neat woman, who never came down to breakfast without her make-up in place and a delicate floral perfume surrounding her. This morning, her usual calm demeanour was gone. She was sitting at her normal table, her lips trembling, her whole body quivering. In her hand, she held a sheet of paper and an unstamped envelope lay next to her plate.

"Why, whatever's the matter, dear?" said Jennie, kneeling beside the frail figure and putting an arm around her trembling shoulders. Melanie opened her mouth a couple of times, but no sound came out. She held out the letter to Jennie. But she was too slow. Flora grabbed it and held it to the light.

"What on earth…" gasped Flora, then she grinned as she began to read the writing on the sheet of cheap, green notepaper. Melanie groaned and buried her face in her hands.

"There was an old lady called Mel
Whose clothes had a terrible smell
She went for a walk…

"Err, that's quite enough, Flora dear – I'm sure Mrs Howells doesn't want her correspondence shared with the whole room" said a quiet voice from the corner table overlooking the rose bed. It was Edith Barstock, a recent arrival at Beehives.

Everyone spun round to look at Edith. It was not the fact that she had challenged Flora – everybody did that. It was the fact that she had spoken at all. In the three months since arriving, Edith had barely opened her mouth – and never once had anybody heard her start a conversation. She was always polite. She would speak if spoken to. But, to be honest, that didn't happen very often. She was yet to be accepted as one of the crowd – or the Honeybee Mafia, as Ted the gardener had been known to call them on occasion.

Beehives was set up in the 1980s. It positioned itself squarely in the middle of the market. Just this side of expensive, so that genteel pensioners, such as retired teachers and civil servants, could afford the fees, but certainly not cheap enough to let in 'the wrong sort of person'. The Trustees (and residents) had a very clear view of the required clientele.

Most of the residents had been there for between five and ten years. There was a sense of routine and certainty to their lives. Everyone had their recognised places in the dining room and their favourite chair in the TV lounge. Coffee was at eleven each morning and tea at four in the afternoon. There was no talking for fifteen minutes, just after seven each evening as they caught up with the goings-on in Ambridge. And there was certainly no possibility of watching Big Brother: "not at all the sort of thing we want to see at our age, dear" stated Maude Rowley when Flora suggested they put it on one night 'just for a laugh'. Maude was the *'Grande Dame'* of Beehives or Queen Bee of the Mafia, depending on your point of view. A large woman, both in stature and personality, she was the font of all knowledge – and arbiter in all disputes. It was Maude who led most conversations. So far, she had failed to find anything of interest to talk about with Edith – so she hadn't bothered. And where Maude led, others followed.

For the rest of the morning, there was only one topic of conversation, Melanie's letter. Who could have sent it? Who would want to upset such a quiet, kindly soul? And for once, Maude had nothing to say. She was as bemused as the rest of them. The recipient herself had retired to her room and refused to come out, even for elevenses.

Around lunchtime, a rumour started to circulate, although no-one knew who had started it. Edith Barstock was believed to have once worked for a private detective. If that was true, maybe she could offer some advice. Surely some of the methods used by her bosses had rubbed off on her?

After lunch, Maude approached the corner table as Edith sat contemplating the roses.

"Edith, dear, I understand that you have some experience of crime scenes" she began. "We're all completely at a loss about this letter of Melanie's – and she's so upset. Is there anything you can do to help?"

Edith smiled. "Well, I was always more of a back-room girl, but of course, I will be delighted to help if I can." Under her gentle guidance, the investigation began. Freda collected copies of everyone's handwriting to compare with that on the letter. It didn't tell them very much as the letter had been typed and only the envelope was handwritten, but it made her feel part of the investigation team.

Gilbert Hodges was adamant that the letter, distinctive in its green envelope, had not been in that morning's pile. They were inclined to believe him. He always had a good look through all the envelopes on the walk up the drive. He had been known to tell people what their mail was about before they had a chance to open it.

Maude herself interviewed Melanie.

"Now Melanie, I know it's distressing for you, but if we are going to solve this little mystery, you really do need to help us. Is there anyone you can think of who might want to upset you in this way? Anyone you've fallen out with recently – or anyone from your past that might be harbouring a grudge?"

Melanie thought hard for a few moments, shook her head with trembling lips – and then collapsed back onto her bed and refused to listen to any more questions.

Next morning, everyone was down in the dining room early, waiting for the post, either with dread or anticipation. But there were no green envelopes that day, or any other day for that matter. Melanie's poem was a one-off that would never be explained.

Later that week, Jennie was updating the residents' database. Smiling, she read two of the entries under "Occupation". Edith Barstock: author and poet and Melanie Howells: actress. Then glancing out of the window to where the Honeybee Mafia were sitting enjoying the autumn sunshine, she smiled once more to see Edith ensconced in the middle of the group, right next to Maude.

12

Mark Never Came Home
Sharon Cook

As soon as he came flying out of the school gates, little Mark badgered his mum to be allowed to go to the fair. For two days it was all he'd talked about. In the end, his mum gave in.

More intent on the telly and arguing with Mark's dad, Maureen would always and forever feel the guilt attached to the moment she said: "Off you go then, you little bleeder. I can't listen to your whining about that bloody fair any longer. Be back by six o'clock."

Giving the seven-year-old some coins to spend, she shouted out: "Make sure you buy some chips out of that."

Maureen lost track of the time. Having spent a good half hour shouting at Mark's dad for drinking three cans of cheap lager by 5pm she'd then cooked sausages for their tea – keeping two back for Mark – before popping out to buy cigarettes. Bumping into a friend on the way back, Maureen had spent a good hour drinking tea at Margery's, each complaining about their respective husbands.

When Maureen arrived home, Mark was nowhere to be found. It was eight o'clock and Maureen was worried.

Sending out Peter, Marks 12-year-old brother, to look for him, Maureen popped to the park behind their house to see if Mark was playing. She'd give him such a rollicking when she found him… The park was empty.

Peter returned, and told his mum that Mark's Chopper bike was chained up to the gatepost of the Carnival Field. Mark was nowhere to be seen.

By nine o'clock Maureen was very worried and woke Mark's dad to tell him the boy wasn't home. The semi comatose fork-lift truck driver growled at her to get the police to find Mark. Well used to his son's regular disappearances, he wasn't bothered. Besides, there was more lager that needed drinking before bed.

Running out to the phone box with no change in her purse – having given it all to Mark – Maureen dialled 999.

"It's my son, he's not home," she blurted out to the voice on the end of the line.

"Now hang on a moment Madam," said the male voice, "do you want police, fire or ambulance?"

"Police, the police. My son, he's not home. It's past 'is bedtime and I don't know where he is. He went to the fair. He's not come home."

Immediately alert, the operator swung into action. "How old is your son, Madam?"

"He's seven. He's only seven and he's at the fair and I can't find 'im. His bike's there, but he's not. He loves that bike. He wouldn't leave it. He, he…"

Stopping the distraught woman's blurting the operator said: "I'm putting you through to the police, Madam. Please, please stay calm. To help find your son you must stay calm. I'm putting you through now. They'll find him love," he added kindly, wondering why a mum would let her seven-year-old child go to the fair on his own.

The town's police station was unmanned after 6pm. By 10 o'clock that night, following the 999 call from Maureen, it was a hub of activity.

Within half an hour there were two police officers standing in Maureen's tiny living room. Mark's dad was sent to bed so they could sit down. (He was happy to go, taking a can of lager with him.)

Having alerted, by radio, the control room, more officers were on their way. By the time Maureen had boiled the first kettle there were four police officers in her home, six searching the fairground, and a further four back at the police station already on the phone to their superiors.

In fact there were so many police cars parked on the double yellow lines by the alleyway, even the non curtain- twitching neighbours were beginning to wonder what was going on.

As a quirk of her neighbourhood, Maureen was well known in the area. She lived with her family in the smallest house in town, which just happened to be in an alleyway situated within the priciest postcode. She didn't shop in Waitrose, didn't drive, smoked like a chimney and was often heard shouting at her children, all three of whom she loved with a ferocity which frequently manifested itself in the school playground if another child upset one of her small clan. In fact, if Maureen had ever been asked to list her hobbies, shouting would most definitely have been at the top of the list.

By 11pm on that June night in 1984 the police had enlisted the help of more than 15 of Maureen's neighbours, several of whom had been caught having more than the one sneaky pint at the Nelson Arms, while out 'walking their dogs'.

The police and their volunteers scoured the Middle England town, just 40 miles to the south of London, but to no avail.

Mark's precious Chopper bike remained chained to the gatepost.

By the following morning Maureen also had a newspaper reporter drinking tea in her living room, warming herself in front of the wall mounted electric heater. Well known to several of the local officers, petite long-haired Shelley Jones was as much a regular feature in town as the police, due to her dedicated crime reporting for the local paper.

If any of them had known, in those early hours, of the horrors that were to follow, no one – not even the most hardened of officers – would have appeared quite so unphased. Everyone assumed Mark would turn up. Everyone, that was, except the senior police officer, who had a distinctly uneasy feeling. The 'golden time' between a disappearance being reported and a search swinging into action was rapidly melting away. And this didn't feel right at all.

Detective Chief Inspector John Marsh was well aware that a major police inquiry, linking four different forces, was currently investigating a number of individuals reportedly on his own patch. He did not like the profiles he had been given, but was not, at this early stage, prepared to pass on information that could freak out his officers, or the family.

Why had the mother let her seven-year-old son go to the fair alone? 'Ye Gods' thought Marsh. Just

seven years old. Trying not to link the intelligence in a
file sitting on his desk with that fact, his blood ran cold.

The tea drinking continued unabated.

As the subsequent police investigations were to
reveal, Mark had indeed disappeared without a trace. It
was as if he had never been to the fair, the only clue
being his beloved Chopper bike.

No one saw him. No one saw him talk to anyone.
No one saw him eating chips, or sweets, or candyfloss.
Not a single fair worker admitted to giving him a ride,
taking money from him, seeing him wandering around or
trying to win a goldfish.

Even headlining the national television news
heralded nothing. The whole town had been aghast about
Mark's unexplained disappearance, but only three phone
calls followed the reconstruction. One from a well
known "character", one from a documented attention
seeker and one from a woman who thought she'd seen a
boy in a blue anorak riding Mark's bike past her window
at 9pm on the night he disappeared.

Further investigations revealed the woman in
question was on medication; and that Mark had never
owned a blue anorak. Besides, his bike had been chained
to the Carnival gatepost. It remained there for three days
before anyone thought to cut it free and send it to
forensics, who found nothing of note.

***

It took more than three years before the investigation hit
a breakthrough.

Shelley had remained fascinated – and remained
friendly – with Maureen. A more unlikely pairing would
have been hard to imagine.

17

But at every twist and turn of the investigation Shelley remained firmly in the background, reporting every development, as well as every non-development. Each anniversary; each time a birthday of Mark's came and went; each time Maureen added another Christmas present to the growing pile in Mark's bedroom - which had become a shrine to the quiet little boy with gammy teeth – Shelly was there. With a photographer, with the family, sometimes with the police.

Even a psychic called, telling Shelley about cold tunnels in a boggy place, a show of strength in sleep, a dark cylinder and dark hazy eyes, four faces; "They were animals" she said. "It was savage" she added. "It was over within two hours" she finished.

Shelley had found out what the file on Marsh's desk contained, after a Christmas night out with some of the investigating team who had off-loaded some of their own horror on to her.

It had only confirmed what she figured most people thought. But Shelley did not pass the information on to the rest of the media, feeling it was inappropriate unless some evidence was found. Why upset Maureen unless there was something concrete to pass on?

But three years after Mark disappeared, in June 1987, several people connected up a number of vital pieces of information. The investigation into Mark's disappearance was re-opened and on a day full of warm summer promise, the town again became the focus of nationwide media attention.

Donning wellies, Shelley accompanied Marsh and his team to a field, up a lane just half a mile from the Carnival ground where Mark had chained his bike. The

Met Police had brought in specialist sniffer dogs, digging teams and so many forensic specialists they were bound to bust the budget.

One national newspaper even hired a helicopter to get a view of the digging. They published pictures, even though Maureen slammed her front door in all the reporters' faces. In fact, Maureen would only speak to Shelley. For almost two months after the failed digging the town's only paper carried a weekly interview with Maureen. Each time she said she just wanted Mark to come home. "I know he's gone," said Maureen, tears welling up. "But I just want to know what happened. I want to bury my son. I want to give him a proper send off. I want 'im safe. I want to know where he is."

Unlike television dramas, the digging revealed nothing. Not a bone, not a shoe, not a tooth – nothing.

When the sniffer dogs had gone, when the news hounds had packed up their notebooks and cameras and told their editors the story was cold, when the senior officers across four police forces had duly received their bollockings for their busted budgets, Shelley carried on drinking tea with Maureen.

Shelley got married, Shelley changed papers, and Shelley moved towns. But still she drank tea with Maureen on a regular basis.

Shelley was determined one day she would reunite Maureen with Mark. There was an answer to the mystery. It was going to be unpleasant, but Maureen needed to know. Shelley also knew that other parents needed to know what happened to seven-year-olds who are left to wander alone – at fairs, in parks, in the countryside, around anonymous streets linked to the highways and byways of a country stalked by men. Men more savagely depraved than starving hyenas or the imaginations of horror flick producers with large budgets.

Shelley knew because Shelley had once been one of those seven-year-old children. Alone. Unprotected. Vulnerable. Shelley was going to find Mark.

At a party one night with her husband, Shelley met a solicitor she knew vaguely through work. Over the wine and the banter the woman told her about a client who 'had a story to tell' (to 'sell', more like, thought Shelley).

A meeting was arranged at the solicitors" office with Patrick Flint, and what Shelley heard made her hackles rise. She somehow remained calm and professional throughout.

Flint had shared a prison cell with a con man. The two men shared rather more than mugs of tea and Flint became the older man's 'wife'. The older man had bragged of his past encounters – and how he would never be caught for what he had done to countless boys the younger the better.

Flint, himself convicted of a string of not-so petty frauds, sensed a commercial opportunity, and milked Sidney Peel for every last drop of information. Now he wanted payback for what he said he had been forced to endure, just to acquire the facts. "I want to put a stop to it all," said Flint, "I still have nightmares about what he told me."

"Give me some names" probed Shelley, so sweetly Flint was hopeful his labours would not be in vain. "I need an advance though" said Flint pitifully. "I have nowhere to live, I have no job and no one wants to employ me." He looked Shelley in the eye: "I need to get some help for what he told me. I can't sleep most nights. I need to be safe before I can talk to you. He's a powerful man and he'll hunt me down."

"We can't make a deal" responded Shelley, touching Flint's arm in a disarmingly gentle fashion, "until I have some hard facts. No editor will believe me.

"Where is little Mark buried?" enquired Shelley.

"How much is a map worth?" asked Flint, who was well practiced at fleecing the lonely and the vulnerable. "Depends where the map leads" countered Shelley, adept at enticing information out of the reluctant.

Flint stated to cry. "I need some help with all this," he sobbed, "it's all too much for one man to carry. You don't know what I had to do to get the information. I need some money, otherwise it means I'm worth nothing."

"Don't worry," said Shelley. "Let's meet again in a month or two and see how you feel then." Flint wiped away the crocodile tears. She was tougher than she looked.

"Hackney Marshes. A series of tunnels linking an old icehouse. Nearby, a well. The house it supplied is gone. I can draw you a map. How much is that worth?

"Was Jonathan there?" asked Shelley, feeling just how enclosed the windowless consulting room actually was.

Flint tried not to look surprised. "And did he ever mention the name Catweazle, or Hissing Sid?"

21

Now it really was cat and mouse, thought Flint. She knew quite a lot. Did that make his information more valuable, or less? How far could he push her before the price went up, or down?

"I'll give you the map" said Flint as he tried not to look her in the face, tried not to lick his lips. "But any more and it's hard cash."

Placing her black pen beside her open notebook, Shelley leant forward across the table, the base of her palms resting on the hard edge. From the corner of her eye she could see the solicitor move slightly forward in her chair by the door, but she said nothing.

"It doesn't work like that Patrick," she whispered. "My paper doesn't pay for stories. We have to sell them to bigger papers. Which means I'm the one who has to convince a bigger editor with lots of money that what you say is true.

"If you want me to put my reputation on the line, I need more than a map drawn by you."

Flint knew exactly who Shelley Jones was. He knew if the reporter closest to the story was believed, he had credibility. He had been a bit too complacent, figured she was a soft touch.

"I've got letters. You can take copies of them." Flint wasn't beaten, but he had to tread carefully. Too much information and he'd blown it. Not enough, and he couldn't reel her in. "But I want police protection."

Sensing a slight advantage, Shelley didn't say a word. Picking up her pen she handed it, along with her open notebook, to Flint. "Draw me the map. I need to make some calls. Can we meet again, tomorrow?"

Flint's solicitor nodded.

Shelley left the building, map in handbag, trying not to shake too much. If she'd played it right...

It was hard persuading the police to take the map seriously. But when they saw photocopies of the letters Peel had written to a number of lovers, four police forces convened a meeting.

By the time the first court case hit the listings, Flint was dead. Killed in a prison shower, after he'd been re-arrested in possession of 15 fake passports following an anonymous tip off. His funeral was a quiet one, just Shelley and his solicitor in attendance. They'd arranged to meet up for a drink anyway; it would have been churlish not to pop into the crematorium on the way.

***

The courts were kept busy for 18 months in all. It was a complex series of cases involving four men and 23 young boys, all under the age of 14 years. Much of what the judges heard was unprintable and, widely agreed, not actually in the public interest.

Sidney Peel – aka Hissing Sid – had worked in fairgrounds most of his sad life. Abused as a young boy by a string of men introduced by a succession of his mother's boyfriends. Peel had grown up with no moral boundaries. His only motivation was of the carnal variety.

Over time he had garnered the support of three other men, each a reject from their own world and each driven by a desire for the company of very young boys. When it wasn't given willingly, the gang took what they wanted by force.

Mark never did make it home.

But his legacy left four evil predators living in fear, behind bars, with only themselves to talk to.

When his dad attempted to sell Mark's Chopper bike as a 'collectable', Maureen divorced him and moved in a toy boy.

The Carnival post became a shrine to hope and misery in equal measure. Strangers left flowers, trinkets and candles. Some left notes of hope, of despair. All remembered Mark.

***

DCI Marsh took early retirement, and started cooking the vegetables he grew. Every night, when Shelley returned home from work, he had a meal on the table for her. And every night they said a silent thank you to Mark, for bringing them together.

The Second Pair of Slippers
Elizabeth Ducie

Olga Petrovna launched herself into the night, leaving behind the warmth of the Metro. She clutched her coat tightly and pulled the fur collar around her ears. The street was almost empty. A last-minute voter hurrying into the polling station; an occasional vehicle passing. But the normal hubbub was missing. The city, exhausted, was resting, holding its breath in anticipation.

As she reached the top of the steps leading to the Elections building, she heard a squeal of tyres on wet tarmac. A Mercedes with blacked-out windows made a rapid U-turn and slammed into the curb, sending droplets of water flying. The doors opened and three large men spilled out. Each wore a discreet earpiece and carried a walkie-talkie. They were followed by a slight figure, wearing an Armani suit, cashmere scarf and overcoat. It was Alexander Ivanovych Polychenko, leading light of the Our Future Party – one of the most well-known men in the country.

The group swept up the steps towards the imposing glass and metal doors, engrossed in their momentum to the exclusion of all else. As they approached, she caught Alexander's eye and smiled, about to say something, to wish him luck. He paused fractionally, but the group was moving too fast and the moment passed. The door swung shut with a hollow clang.

Olga stared after the group, but all she could see was her reflection in the glass. Her face seemed frozen. More of a grimace than a smile. Slowly, like snow in the sunshine, it melted, replaced by a look of disappointment. She clenched her fists, biting back angry words. She was wearing her best suit and new boots; her hair was freshly bleached and permed. But to them, she didn't exist.

Olga compared the man now with the boy she first knew so many years ago. They lived in the same apartment block, attended the same school. In the summer evenings they sat on the swings in the small courtyard, surrounded by crumbling balconies, and planned their futures. They wandered hand-in-hand down Leninsky Boulevard. There was no McDonalds, no internet cafes and most of the shop windows were empty. But, each evening, there were crowds of people strolling in the fading light. Even in those dark days, they were free to walk and think.

Following the group into the building on that Sunday night, Olga heard the clock strike nine. She reached into her bag for an official pass. It was time for her to work.

***

Monday lunchtime, Olga walked through the dim building towards the canteen, ignoring the crowd that milled around her, demanding answers. Only three of the eight light fittings contained bulbs. After the bright atmosphere in her office and the counting hall, she had difficulty focusing in the semi-darkness.

As she opened the door she smelt the usual aroma of a municipal canteen; a subtle mix of fat that has been fried once too often - and dill. Dill, the aromatic herb used to flavour everything – fish, meat, sauces and mashed potato.

Lights flickered from all sides. Wall-mounted TVs in opposite corners of the room showed different channels. One an old Russian movie, the other a local fashion programme with skeletal models showing last year's designs. No-one was watching either. People were concentrating on their food, enjoying a brief respite from the mayhem in the rest of the building.

She chose a chopped beetroot salad from the display cabinet, added to her tray some vinegary rye bread and a glass of raspberry compote and moved with leaden feet to an empty table. As she passed a mirror on the wall, she glanced furtively at her reflection. Her boots, all pointed toe and high heel, still shone. But they'd rubbed a blister on her left heel and she was beginning to wish she'd chosen a pair a little less fashionable and a little more comfortable. The adrenaline rush provided by the excitement of the occasion, and her role in it, had started to wear off. She looked at the sleepy women serving the food and sympathised with their yawns. If this went on much longer, she would have to close the canteen for the staff to get some rest.

As she ate, she glanced across to the glass-walled section reserved for the politicians. There, at the centre table sat Alexander Ivanovych and his supporters. She was still hurting from their slight, although the sting had faded somewhat.

The four men were smoking and drinking small glasses of vodka. In front of them lay the remains of Russian salad and aubergine rolls. Their jackets had been slung over the backs of their chairs and their ties had come adrift. Their posture was tense, their brows creased and they kept looking towards the door. Alexander was

27

talking urgently and waving his hands around. First one
man rose from the table, then another. They walked out
of the canteen in the direction of the counting hall. After
a few minutes, the third companion followed them.
Alexander chewed moodily on a fingernail, tapping his
foot in a staccato manner. Then, he too jumped to his
feet and left.

For ten minutes or more, the tableau remained
unchanged; a table bearing the debris of a meal in
progress. Finally, Alexander came back into the room.
He took his former place at the head of the table and
smoked yet another cigarette. Eventually, one of the
others returned. By the time Olga left the canteen, the
other two men had still not re-appeared. She was to see
them later in the company of a young up-and-coming
politician from a rival party.

***

On Tuesday morning, for the second day in a row, Olga
stared out of her office window at the slow dawn. Light
was creeping across the street, turning the snow from
grey to brown. It had been many months since any white
had shown through the lingering piles pushed by the
snowploughs to the sides of the road. Her eyes were
stinging from lack of sleep and she was having difficulty
concentrating. She hauled herself to her feet and checked
her reflection in the mirror once more. Her skirt looked
like she had slept in it. Strictly speaking, she had – but
only for a few moments just after midnight when she
could no longer stay awake. Her blouse looked as if it
had never been near an iron. If she had known the
counting was going to take this long, she would have
brought a spare with her.

Nevertheless, she knew her big moment had arrived at last. The counting was finally complete. Every objection and argument had been dealt with. All parties accepted the results and the official announcement could now be made.

Olga applied a new coat of lipstick and checked that none was smeared on her front teeth. In the early morning light, the gold replacements for her top molars shone dully. She threw back her shoulders, took a deep breath, picked up the document from her desk and opened the door.

It was strangely silent. For the past thirty-two hours, reporters had hounded her each time she ventured out of the office. Whenever she went to the canteen or the counting hall, she was followed by her own personal pack.

"Olga Petrovna, is there any news?"

"Not yet – we've just gone to a third recount"

"But can you tell us who you think will win? Anything for the early edition?"

"Sorry gentlemen. I can't help you. You know I can't say anything until the final result is announced."

This time, the corridor was empty. As she passed the open door of the pressroom, she realised why. All around the room, representatives of the local and international media were sleeping. One had made a bed out of cushions and lay stretched across the floor. A couple were lying with their heads on the desks.

'Just like Alexander and me when we were in junior school' she thought.

The others were hunched in their chairs, trying to find a comfortable position. She rapped smartly on the doorframe.

"Gentlemen of the press - official announcement in five minutes". She smiled to herself as she walked on, leaving behind a sense of panic and urgency.

As Olga walked on to the stage, she glanced at the paper in her hand. For each result, she had underlined the successful name in red, to make sure there were no mistakes. Under the heading of Central Oblast, the name she had underlined was Yulia Grigorovna Semerenko. The difference between her votes and those of Alexander had been very small. That was one of the reasons why this election night had gone on for so very long.

Olga glanced up and saw Alexander standing at the back of the room. He was wearing his jacket once more, but his tie had gone - and so had all his companions. Mentally, she compared how he looked now with the last time he had appeared on television, at an election rally a few days ago. Supporters and well-wishers had surrounded him. But he was irritable with the crowds, his answers to questions off-hand and dismissive. She remembered wondering where this streak of arrogance had come from. Didn't he know that he depended on these people, rather than the other way around?

For a brief moment, she allowed her neutrality to slip and found to her surprise she was pleased he had lost. Maybe it was the lingering effect of Sunday night's slight. Maybe she had not liked the man she had watched on TV, the man he had become.

As the television lights shone down on her and the cluster of microphones pointed upwards from the front of the stage, Olga announced to the country the results of the election for Parliamentary Deputies. She leaned slightly against the lectern to support her weary body and was thankful that her feet were hidden. It would not do for the news footage to show that the Head of the Central Elections Commission had made her announcement in fluffy pink slippers – having finally abandoned her new boots as the mistake she had known them to be, even as she bought them.

***

As Olga walked out of the building some hours later, she was hit by an icy blast of wind. She paused to tighten her scarf around her neck and pull her gloves up to cover her wrists. She was suddenly aware of someone at the bottom of the steps. A slight figure, still expensively dressed but looking very crumpled and somehow older. He was wearing the cashmere scarf around his neck, but his overcoat hung over one arm. He shivered in the cold. No longer entitled to an official car and without his former bodyguards, he seemed uncertain what to do or where to go.

She slowly walked down the steps towards the man. At the sound of her heels on the stone, he looked up and recognition broke through the bewilderment in his eyes.

"They don't want me anymore. It's all been for nothing".

Olga gazed at him and the final vestiges of hurt and anger melted away. She no longer saw Alexander Ivanovych, an arrogant politician wound up in himself and his ambitions. She didn't even see the little boy who excitedly told her his dreams as they wandered the streets. She just saw Sasha, a husband, father and grandfather who had for a while lost sight of what was really important and now needed support and reassurance.

Reaching the bottom of the steps, she slipped her arm through his and leaned over to kiss his cold cheek.

"Come home Sasha" she said. "I have your slippers warming by the fire and Anna is bringing the babies to see us today."

No Buttonholes Today
Sharon Cook

The dress hung on its heavily padded hanger, dominating the small bedroom.

Laid out on the single bed along one side of the room were an array of accessories which would elevate the couture creation from a pale, yet elegant silk shift dress to a bridal vision.

Shoes dyed to match the exact shade of 'oyster', a delicate bespoke tiara, beaded hairgrips, a short veil fashioned from antique lace and an exquisite cream lace bra and matching knickers.

Stockings – hold ups of course, nothing should be allowed to interfere with the smooth lines of such a beautifully simple garment – almost completed the *ensemble*.

A blue garter from her girlie friends and a diamond brooch, which had belonged to Eleanor's grandmother, would furnish the image with everything needed to ensure Eleanor looked stunning.

As she stood contemplating the items before her Eleanor heard her mother: "Tea or coffee love?" followed by a swift "Or something stronger?" from her dad.

Smiling at their predictability Eleanor gratefully accepted a mug of coffee (deftly laced with brandy from her father's hip flask, both of them grinning at their complicity).

"Now come on love, we can't be late today. Today of all days. Do you want a hand?" fussed Anne, mother-of-the-bride. "I'll be ready in two ticks. I can do up your zip for you."

"It's Ok mum. I'll give you a shout when I need a hand," replied Eleanor.

Standing, staring at the scene before her, Eleanor didn't know whether to laugh or cry.

How had all this happened? And so quickly? Out of nowhere!

One minute your life is sussed and then 'Boom!', all change.

And now here she was. 'The Big Day'. A day like no other. A day that could change her future forever. Take her places she had never been before.

Or maybe not. Maybe everything would stay the same, but better.

Still, day dreaming at this stage was not wise. 'Come on girl' Eleanor cajoled herself and within 10 minutes she was dressed and calling for her mum to come and zip her up.

Eleanor walked down the stairs, to sighs, gasps and a 'wow!' from Uncle Matthew. Then the immaculately dressed family was whisked off in a flurry of the town's finest taxis.

Standing together in the family living room, father turned to daughter: "Are you sure this is what you want love? It's not too late you know."

"Oh dad. Thank you! I'm fine." And Eleanor smiled at her dad as he poured them each a very large one from the not-so-secret bottle in the sideboard.

The car arrived, the pair set off and during the ten minute ride little was said, the tension mounting.

As her dad opened the door for Eleanor she could see the crowds on the steps. Several photographers surged forward and she was momentarily bedazzled by the flash guns clicking away.

A uniformed guard came rushing forward and shooed the snappers away as Eleanor and her father ascended the court house steps.

Once inside Eleanor was ushered into a side room as her family took their seats.

By the time the judge had entered his domain, Eleanor was ensconced in the dock, flanked by two rather bemused female prison officers.

As the High Court Judge, heavily robed in red, peered at Eleanor across the top of his bookish spectacles, the clerk – for such a grand occasion wearing a wig himself – asked the defendant to rise.

"Are you Eleanor Suzanne Richmond?"

"Yes, My Lord", she replied, quite meekly.

"You are charged that on June 9 2010, you did attack Mr Robert Michael Thomas with an ice pick, with intent to cause him grievous bodily harm. How do you plead? Guilty? Or Not Guilty?"

"Not Guilty" responded Eleanor.

The following three hours involved so much legal speak Eleanor thought she was must be speaking a different language.

Fortunately Eleanor's eminent barrister was able to communicate the gist to the judge.

It transpired – and this all before a jury was sworn in to make judgement – that on June 10 2010 Eleanor had been due to marry the aforementioned alleged victim.

Popping round to his house to finalise the button holes with her then-fiancé, she had found him in bed with, not just the local barmaid, but the barmaid's rather buxom cousin as well.

Consumed by a welter of emotions (including rage, jealousy, bemusement, betrayal and failure) Eleanor grabbed the nearest thing to hand – Rob's ice pick from the top of his mountaineering kit – and hurled it at him with all her might. It connected with the top of his right thigh. Eleanor, still being connected to the ice pick, ensured it buried itself with much more force. The pick hit a main artery and blood went everywhere. Only the quick thinking of Rob's best man saved the situation – and Rob – by calling an ambulance so swiftly.

When all the wailing and shouting and screaming had died down Eleanor was arrested, and eventually charged.

Despite his reputation as the town's Lothario, Rob's injuries had to be taken seriously by the police.

Eleanor, devastated by the turn of events, vowed to have her day in court. "Shame to waste the dress entirely," she told her mum.

So she decided the jury might have more sympathy if they saw before them a woman scorned rather than a mad, angry attacker.

No jury ever got to see the dress.

The judge threw the case out.

Eleanor walked free from court, without a stain on her character.

And straight into the arms of the best man.

Dragon Flags
Elizabeth Ducie

The day after the accident, Meg returned from boarding school. Climbing out of the car she stood tall, throwing back her shoulders. But she was biting her lip and balling her hands into tight fists. Then she ran into the house. Ever since, she has been shut in her room, listening to CDs and texting her friends. She's hardly eaten a thing.

At seven, Matthew is still my little boy. After school, he sits in the garden with his books. He pretends to read, but I don't see him turning many pages.

There were so many places Joel and I planned to take our kids. Swimming with dolphins, sailing around the Greek islands, on safari, even visiting Santa Claus in Lapland. Somehow, we never got round to it.

Joel's office is in the Folly in our garden; the wooden, upside-down hut built as a guest house. Downstairs, the bedroom; upstairs his studio, reached by an external staircase. With windows on all sides, he called it his dragon lookout post.

He devised a system of signals, small flags hoisted from the balcony. Red meant 'man at work – disturb on pain of being eaten by dragons!' Yellow was 'man needing sustenance – bring coffee and chocolate biscuits, then retreat before dragons return.' The one the children really loved was the green one: 'dragons sleeping – man requiring company'. There was also a purple flag, the Dragon Veto. The children waved this from their windows in case of emergency. 'Forget about dragons – we need help.'

Now, outside the church, I watch Meg blink
furiously, surreptitiously wiping lipstick off her cheek
and I think about her first encounter with death. Aged
four, she won a goldfish at the fair. Knowing these fish
rarely survive, we reluctantly bought a bowl and fish
food. 'Goldie' was installed on a shelf in Meg's
bedroom. We hoped her enthusiasm would wane before
the inevitable. Two weeks later, we were awakened by a
howl from our daughter's room.

"Mummeeeeeee! Goldie's drownded!"

We just managed to stop Meg attempting mouth-
to-mouth resuscitation. While I explained about God
needing pets for company, Joel found a suitable box.
Below the cherry tree we started our pet cemetery.

As the well-wishers pass, Matthew stands with
his head high, taking each hand offered, ignoring the
tears on his cheeks. When he was born, his granny
knitted him a blue teddy, with a well-rounded tummy
and a tendency to fall on its face. Over time, Boo Bear
became worn and grubby. Stitches came loose and were
redone. Stuffing popped out under his arm. Once, I
washed him; his ears stretched to twice their size, one of
his legs got twisted in the tumble dryer – and Matthew
wouldn't speak to me for a week.

One day we went to the park for the afternoon.
We played catch and tag, ate ice-creams, fed the ducks
and had our tea under the chestnut trees. Finally, we
went for a row on the lake. By the time we had finished,
the sun was starting to sink, Matthew was fast asleep and
even Meg looked heavy-eyed. Next morning we realised
Boo Bear had been left behind. When the boating
attendant arrived, we were waiting for him. We searched

every boat, but it was no good. Matthew didn't cry, just went quiet for several days. When granny offered to knit him a new bear, he shook his head with a sad look – the same look I see now.

For Meg, who currently favours Goth, black is not unusual. What is new is the manner in which she wears these sombre clothes. Her hair is tied back with black ribbon. Her blouse is pressed; her skirt hangs modestly just below the knee and she has forsaken her Converse All Stars for a pair of patent shoes.

Matthew is less compliant. He wears a clean pair of trousers and a dark sweatshirt, but is adamant in his refusal to be parted from his trainers. It doesn't offend me, and Joel has never paid attention to what the kids are wearing, but our son may need shielding from elderly relatives before the day is out.

The service is poignant and slips by in a flash. Friends and family members have chosen readings, some sacred, some not, which have special meaning for us. Matthew reads a story he wrote last Christmas – 'Why My Family Is The Best'. His voice is rough, as though starting a cold, but he continues. Finally, his voice fades; he chokes on the words. His sister walks to his side, reads the last sentences and takes him back to his seat. I feel a prickle of tears as pride wells within me.

In the old part of the cemetery, gravestones have been eaten by the wind and rain; few of the names are readable. Walkways between the graves are sunken; monuments tower above them and lean over as though to shake hands with their neighbours. In the newer section, graves are grassed over, with just headstones to mark each resting place.

At the graveside, I wonder what future paths my children will take. Fear clutches at me as I think of the perils they face. Then, I remind myself that at some point we have to let them go; like the sparrows I watch each spring, training their fledglings.

Over the years, Meg has fluctuated between the humanitarian and the commercial. I'm not sure what she wants to do at present, but I know it involves rock music, friends in the media – and working nights.

Matthew is too young to make plans. For him, the end of term play is as far as his horizons stretch.

In truth, I don't really mind what my children do with their lives. I just want them to be as happy as Joel and I were. Along with the studying and hard work, I hope they will find time to meet and recognise the people who will make their lives complete.

Finally, when everyone is in place, the vicar speaks.

"We therefore commit her body to the ground; earth to earth, ashes to ashes, dust to dust; in the sure and certain hope of the Resurrection to eternal life."

Looking down on the coffin, I see the plaque: Sally Josephine Broome. It had happened so quickly, driving home in the twilight, Joel by my side. A dark shape launched itself out of the roadside trees, pulling up yards from the car, its fiery eyes reflecting the headlights. I heard Joel shout.

"What the hell is that?"

"Some kind of animal… I'm going to hit it … oh no" I was fighting to turn the wheel. At the last minute, the car swerved to one side. Unable to stop in time, I saw the bonnet crumple and come towards me as we smashed into a tree. The windscreen exploded and the headlights went out.

"Sally, my God, Sally" I heard Joel shout, but faintly. Everything flickered to a halt and there was silence. Then, as though the clock had restarted, the beast gave a snort and disappeared back into the wood. I found myself watching as ambulances came and went. And I have been watching ever since – witness to everything, but unable to take part or give comfort.

"Goodbye mummy" I hear the children whisper as the words of the service fade and they walk away. Suddenly they pause, look at each other, then turn to wait for the tall, sombre figure limping behind them. Joel was luckier than I. He escaped with a broken ankle and bruising.

Last night, I watched as my husband sat first with Meg and then with Matthew, keeping them company and helping them through their hurt.

Meg had bright spots on her cheeks and she kept dragging her hair out of her eyes.

"How could she do it? Wasn't she looking where she was going? Had she been drinking? Why weren't you driving – you know she gets tired when she's driving at night!"

The questions and accusations tumbled from her lips as she strode around the room. Joel didn't try to answer. He just sat patiently, waiting for our daughter to calm down. Finally, she threw herself on the bed, burying her head in the pillow, shoulders heaving. Joel reached over to stroke her hair.

"She was paying attention, poppet. If she hadn't, she would have kept going and hit the animal. It made her jump – but she tried to save it from getting hurt – and the car went out of control. I know you're angry and if it helps, you can take it out on me. Maybe I should have offered to drive. But don't blame your mother. I want you to remember her with kindness and love, not anger."

Later, at bedtime, Matthew's room was empty, the bed untouched. Joel found him asleep in the Folly, curled up like a dormouse on the bed. He clutched a scrap of purple cloth in his fist and there were streaks of dried tears on his cheeks. As Joel carried him back to the house, our son stirred.

"What did I do wrong, daddy? Why did mummy die? Was she cross with me?"

"No, darling, your mummy loved you very much, She was never cross with you for long. She was very proud of you. She died because of an accident, not your fault; not anybody's fault."

When the house was dark and quiet, I gazed at my children's faces in sleep and hoped they would realise that Joel is also hurting. He too needs comforting.

Now, as my husband catches up with them, they smile and each takes hold of one of his hands. I feel the bond between us stretching to breaking point, while the one between them strengthens and tightens. It is time to say goodbye. As my sight fades, I am comforted by the thought that the three most important people in my life will find the strength to carry on. But I think the purple flag is going to get plenty of use in the coming months.

The Living Room
Sharon Cook

The living room had always looked pristine.

Every time Soula passed the window, she took a sneaky peek. The curtains were always open during the day; and each day the room looked utterly beautiful.

In the winter, as the dark evenings silently claimed the season, new aspects of the room came into focus. Shady corners were lit by subtle, luscious lights, each clearly placed to highlight another beautiful object. An Art Deco lamp, Georgian silverware, heavy glass candlesticks, a Victorian planter graced with a 'Mother-in-Laws Tongue', a display cabinet full of elegant china.

Always clean, with a tasteful neutral palette showcasing the expensive antique furniture which oozed taste and extravagance, the room was a magazine page gilded with wordy outpourings. Soula could almost smell the beeswax built up over years of polishing.

Even the cushions had the look of designer creations.

Soula had no idea if it was a 'she', a 'he' or a 'they' who lived within its confines.

Assuming the room's creator – or creators – worked in the city, as most people in the village did, Soula confined her nosiness to the sitting room she had grown to love over the three years she had been walking past it.

Being rather more charity shop than boutique Soula's own living room was somewhat shabby – without the chic. Yes, it was clean. But with little money and three-year-old twins to care for, Soula's horizons

43

were seriously limited. Gawping through the window of the house next-door-but-one gave her a very real thrill, probably because it gave her a sense of belonging somewhere.

Just as Tilly and George had come into the world, their provider had departed. Not to a better place, but to a better job.

He returned three or four times a year; to sort out paperwork, take photographs of the twins and make sure Soula was OK – though what that meant she no longer knew. Tilly and George had made their calm and unhurried appearance into an uncertain world just four days after Soula had married Adam.

Each time Adam re-appeared he would assure Soula everything was OK, leave her a new address and phone number – to be used for emergencies only! – and, after a week or so, he would be gone again.

Soula didn't ask how long the set up would last. She knew she had shelter, warmth and food for the twins and herself. It may have been a lonely and confusing life at times, but it was a hell of a lot better than her previous existence, before Adam had found her. For that alone she assumed she must love him and because she loved him, she must trust him – as he had told her to do.

So it was on with the daily rituals of looking after Tilly and George, which she loved, domesticity, which she also loved, and living on a tight budget – which she was very good at.

Apart from books, television and the radio, the 'living room' was her distraction.

Popping out to buy a bag of rice one afternoon, Soula couldn't help but notice something was different as she peeked through one of the wooden sash windows.

Papers and books were scattered across the floor, several mugs adorned the central coffee table and it looked as if the sumptuous cushions were totally unplumped.

Such was her practiced eye, she had taken the changes in as she scuttled past the house, whose front door, just as her own, opened straight onto the pavement.

'How odd', thought Soula, determined to take a much closer look on the way back.

Intrigued by the changes, Soula couldn't sleep that night.

The following day she attempted to linger in front of the window by attending to the zips on both her children's coats.

There was even more disarray. Dirty plates and takeaway containers stood next to yesterday's mugs, and the contents of a carrier bag were scattered across one of the three sofas. An obviously-read newspaper, leaflets spilling out of a plastic wallet, empty carrier bags and the cream carpet confettied with what looked like screwed up till receipts. A pair of men's shoes was lying by the door, a large coat was draped across the arm of the *chaise longue* and a pile of half-folded washing teetered perilously close to the edge of a large, green wing chair.

Returning minutes later with two onions, a bag of carrots and some dried chick peas, Soula again feigned coat fiddling techniques to get a better look. This time she was really concerned. Had the house been burgled? Was someone ill?

For two more days she worried as the mess got worse – ruling out a burglary, but surely increasing the chance of illness.

By now a pile of books had fallen over by the fireplace, a couple of cookery books lay open on the carpet beside them, a pile of unopened post – some in coloured envelopes – and more rifled-through newspapers added to the *mêlée*. Filled carrier bags with unfamiliar designer names were piled up by the glass fronted display cabinet. The antique china show-cased within taking second stage to several large, unmarked, brown cardboard boxes stacked against the wall.

Soula found it all quite shocking. Never before had she seen more than one newspaper abandoned to yesterday's news. Or books casually discarded.

The oak (she presumed) shelves at the far end of the room were always neat. Now they looked more like an earthquake had ripped through them.

Yet Soula couldn't knock on the door and ask if everything was OK. Apart from being too shy she had no idea who lived there, and, quite frankly, she knew her grasp of the English language wouldn't stretch to polite conversation. Besides, the house owner, or owners, would know she had been examining their living room in minute detail.

En route to buy some chillies, fresh ginger and coriander on day four, the penny dropped.

By the following day her suspicions were confirmed.

Seeing an open packet of nappies scattered across the carpet by the fireplace – competing for space with the pile of books - numerous packets of wet wipes, muslins, a baby car seat and a stack of tiny baby grows by the coffee table, it was obvious. The living room had a baby!

Opening her own front door with a big smile Soula laughed, and by the time her happy little twins were tucked up in bed later that night she couldn't believe how silly she had been – or how long it had taken her to work out what had happened.

When Tilly and George were born Adam had been a great help. At the birth he had done all the right things, massaged the right places and been so tender and gentle with the babies that Soula had wept with joy on a daily basis.

But after 10 days of 'fatherhood' Adam had told Soula he had to go, that he had to earn money and that she would not see him for long periods of time. "Trust me", Adam had said. "You are safe. There will be money" he had added. She had trusted him, the man who had rescued her. She was safe. Money arrived in the bank each month. It was as he had said. And if she was lonely and confused, she looked to Tilly and George for comfort. People in the village were not unfriendly, but she knew no one.

Besides, Adam would be home again soon. Maybe this time he would be staying? She knew so little about him, yet she owed him everything.

Their eyes had met across a crowded refugee camp, through his camera lens.

47

Soula"s entire family had been wiped out in a rebel raid. Her home – inhabited by four generations – was razed to the ground. Soula had fled before she, too, was shot.

She had not escaped further atrocities, yet her grief had been tempered by an existence powered purely by survival.

It had taken Soula almost two weeks to reach a refugee camp, where a number of international aid agencies had scooped her up and plastered over the gashes, the grazes and the knife wounds. The internal injuries had healed, over time. The antibiotics had probably saved her life. None of the medics who had revived the nineteen-year-old could believe any baby – let alone two – could have survived.

When Adam had met Soula, seven months after her escape, he was moved not just by her unimaginable story, but by something he just couldn't understand. His hardened war photographers shell served him well. Nothing ever got inside. Not fear, not compassion, not anger. His entire life revolved around the click of the shutter. An almost primeval urge to capture what would shock most, what would tell the world most how pointless war actually is.

Yet he had been drawn into this young woman's life. He lost sleep. More worryingly, he lost pictures.

The international press pack he hung around with was astonished when Adam announced he was taking Soula back to the UK with him. "Bloody hell mate" laughed Australian Bill, "keep it in your trousers. Plenty of other women around. No need to hitch up with damaged goods."

"Are you mad?" said his news editor, tucked up in an air conditioned ninth floor office. "Mind you, she'll make a good bit of copy for the Saturday mag," he'd added, brightening. "Get plenty of pics of 'er in the refugee camp, cooking or something. Make sure there's plenty of ragged looking kids in the background," he added, for good measure.

"Well don't expect me to help," said Adam's mum, "I've got far too much to do looking after your dad - and running the business. In case you'd forgotten." His mother's disapproval was never lacking. Adam had learnt to dodge the emotional grenades, mostly by ignoring his highly privileged, dysfunctional family.

Pulling in every favour he would ever be owed, Adam secured papers for Soula and strapped her in beside him on the Hercules jet back to England. The RAF never knew the young woman with beautiful brown eyes was so heavily pregnant.

War obscures reason, a Press Card opens doors and confidence masks untold truths. All this Adam knew.

He also understood that damaged people knew how to survive.

Adam's focus centred on his innate ability to capture shocking moments in time, regardless of personal risk. Soula buried her own survival instincts deep within her primeval need to mother.

Hearing the cry of a tiny baby and a mother's sobbing prompted Soula to knock on the front door of the house next-door-but-one.

Greeted by a woman in her mid thirties, wiping her eyes while attempting to dab baby sick off the front of a very expensive looking, milk-stained silk shirt, Soula smiled. Anna introduced herself. Soula had entered the hallowed living room - and she was about to drink tea within its confines!

Within the week Adam was home. A bullet through his left leg, sustained in a Libyan rebel stronghold, had forced him away from the front line.

Soula put him to bed, administered prescriptions and bought him new pyjamas.

Adam succumbed. To pain, to fear, to home-made chicken soup and the attentions of two very inquisitive, three-year-old twins.

He also succumbed to clean Egyptian cotton sheets, reviving herbal teas and the peace and tranquillity of English birdsong. Then he started to cry. For two days Adam buried himself in grief.

An expert in such matters Soula moved around her husband, the unknown man in her bed, simply ministering. Loving him with her home-cooked food and her unquestioning loyalty.

When Adam stopped crying he told Soula he had been shot while trying to rescue a three-year-old boy. He realised, he told his beautiful wife, he needed to start living his own life. He needed his own home. And for the first time ever, Soula and Adam embraced.

Hazelnuts and Marble Chips
Elizabeth Ducie

We stand at the check-in desk, the crowd swirling around us. Momma sobs, her weather-beaten face looking older than I have ever seen it. Masha's cheeks are a fiery red, but at least she has stopped shouting at me. She bites her lip and tries to hide the single tear rolling down her cheek. Even Baba Maria, who survived the hunger of the 1930s and the Great Patriotic War, looks as though this single act of mine is one treachery too far.

Uncle Leo is stoic. He gazes around the entrance hall, seeing it for the first time. Brown marble pillars support a dome painted pale blue with a cream garland at the base. It reminds me of the English vase in the local museum – a present from a visiting politician. The frieze around the walls shows scenes of rural and industrial life – reflections of old Lugansk. All flights are listed on a single board. Nine destinations per week and one of those is Kiev. I have a ticket for Kiev in my hand.

My family are each dealing in their own way with the news I gave them only last night, when it was too late for them to do anything about it.

Now I'm leaving home, it will be hard for everyone. Baba Maria will have no one to carry her shopping. Uncle Leo will have no help on the farm – and he finds it more difficult each year. Little Masha will have no one to tell her stories to. But I think it is Momma who will suffer the most. She spends her days keeping house, washing clothes or preparing dinner for when I get in. She tells the neighbours her son is so good to her, such an honourable man. If only she knew.

I needed to tell them I was going to leave. I didn't need to tell them I might never come back. I couldn't tell them I was going for work. I have a job here, and although times are hard, we're surviving. I couldn't tell them I was ill. Momma would want me to be nursed here, or she would try to come with me. I couldn't tell them I was going to get married. It is impossible that I would marry a strange girl in a faraway place without bringing her home to live. I could tell them I am going away to train, maybe as a veterinarian; but they know I hate to study and have never passed any exams in my life.

Maybe I should have slipped away without telling them anything? Instead, I told the truth. At least, some of it.

***

It all started when we were lads, going to the local school. Ivan and I were rivals in everything. Who could pitch a stone furthest, run the fastest, or score the most goals. We both wanted to be the next Oleg Blokhin. Our rivalry was healthy, not bitter. We were fairly evenly matched. He was slight and wiry, so did best at speed games. What I lacked in speed, I made up for in strength. We didn't compete in the classroom. At that time, neither of us had any interest in learning.

We only fell out once – and it was her fault. She arrived at our school when we were nine. She was tiny, with long glossy hair, the colour of the chestnuts that fall from the trees each autumn. Her eyes were the colour of hazelnuts and always held a smile.

She had been to school in Kiev before moving to

52

Lugansk and was really smart. She could answer all the
questions, although she never pushed herself forward.
The tales she wrote in composition class were magical –
and she never got less than 9 out of 10 in the maths tests.

She lived next door to me, so the teacher gave
her Ivan's seat. We became instant friends and would
talk all the way home each afternoon. Ivan never waited
for us. He said he had to help his mother in the shop,
and ran off as soon as the school bell rang each day. My
new friend and I were so wrapped up in each other; I
didn't have time to think there might be any other
reason.

Her father was an engineer, working on a
construction site just outside town. Within three months,
the Soviet Union was dead and, for the moment, so was
his project. In Ukraine we were learning to walk on our
own once more and had other priorities. Her family
moved back to Kiev and our brief time together was
over.

Months later, as the temperature dropped, the
leaves turned brown and the summer was little more than
a warm glow, Ivan told me there was another reason he
hadn't hung around after school that summer.

"Boy, I'm glad that little cow's gone back to
Kiev," he growled. "She couldn't play football – so you
didn't play football. She couldn't run fast – so you
stopped running. When she tried to pitch a stone, she
looked like a ruptured duck, so you stopped pitching
stones. You're much more fun again now she's not
here."

It was as though he had thrown icy water in my
face. I was unable to think straight. I wanted to tell my

friend he was mistaken. If he'd had a chance to get to know her, he would have thought differently. Somehow, I couldn't find the words. Very soon, the moment passed and it was too late.

In the years that followed, our friendship strengthened. It survived the time when Ivan was away, studying in the Engineering Institute in Kharkov. He came home rarely, but we always managed to meet up and relive old times over several glasses of vodka.

Now Ivan is back for good, engineering abandoned as he runs the shop his late mother left him. His new wife is settling in well. She remembers little of her previous visit to this part of the country. No longer tiny, her hair still has reflections of chestnuts in autumn and her eyes are still hazel.

***

This much I told them last night as the fire died down and the dogs, tired out from chasing rabbits, shadows and their own tails, snoozed on the hearth rug. About the time we met by chance as she was coming out of the shop a few weeks ago. I didn't tell them about all the other times I was walking past "by chance" when she came out, nor the time we danced at the village social. I held her so tightly she begged me to let her breathe. Nor about the time I tried to kiss her when she was sitting in her garden waiting for Ivan to come back from the wholesalers. Most of all, I didn't talk about the change in her eyes. The sparkling warmth has left them when they look at me. They seem more like marble chips from the pillars surrounding us in this airport entrance.

Once through check-in, I wander around the stark departure hall. No murals or other decoration here, just

54

black and white marble, a few chairs. Through the
window, I see the old trucks carrying baggage to the
only plane parked on the airfield. People sit quietly,
trying not to meet one another's gaze. The silence is
oppressive; the walls too close. My breaths are shallow. I
try the door at the end of the hall, which leads out onto
the tarmac. But it is still locked.

For now, I can go neither forward nor back.

How Does Your Garden Grow?
Sharon Cook

"**M**um! Mum!" shouted the small boy with the snotty nose. "Mum," he added for the most annoying of entrances, finally skidding to a halt by the kitchen sink.

"Yes love," said Rita, a smile lighting up her care worn face. Removing her reddened hands from a bowl of particularly hot washing-up water, the woman dried them off on the apron she was wearing over a faded summer print dress, and hugged her eight-year-old son.

"Now then Daniel. What's the question?"

"How did you know I was going to ask you a question?" laughed the little boy as his mum deftly wiped his nose on a piece of kitchen paper.

"Because you're very good at asking questions," smiled his mum, somewhat wearily.

"I like questions. And granddad said it's about learning. And I've got homework," he added proudly, for good measure.

"Come on then," said Rita, "What's your question?"

"Mum. What's it like falling in love?" asked Daniel, breathlessly.

Somewhat taken aback, Rita was momentarily lost for words.

"Well, she stalled, "well – why do you want to know?"

"It's for homework mum," grinned Daniel. "We have to write about what love is. If I don't know how you fall in love, how can I write what love is?"

56

The child's logic was heartbreaking in its simplicity.

"Well. Um, love is complicated Daniel," thought Rita out loud.

"Yes mum, but how do you 'fall in love'?" persisted Daniel.

"It's not as simple as that my darling boy," smiled Rita. "No one really knows 'how' to fall in love. It just happens. I fell in love with you the second you were born. And I've loved you ever since. Every minute of every day."

"But I'm your son. You love me anyway. You tell me all the time. How did it feel when you fell in love with dad?" Daniel ploughed on.

"That's a very good question." Pausing for a moment of wistful contemplation – Daniel could tell his mum was thinking – the silence seemed to go on a long time.

At last Rita opened her mouth and said: "It felt good. It's a warm feeling. It feels safe Daniel, like you know something is just right."

"Thanks mum. I can write down good and warm and safe. That's brilliant, thanks mum!" and Daniel was off.

Standing by the sink Rita smiled to herself. It had been good – once. She had felt safe and warm – once.

Seduced by Daniel's father at just 17, Rita had felt all those things. And more. But she had, she was ashamed to admit now, also fallen for his matinee idol looks, his car and the fact he was five years older and earned a good living as a printer's apprentice.

Now in her forties – Daniel had been a late surprise after years of infertility heartache – Rita often reflected on love. Mills and Boon books were her secret vice. The slushy books kept her dream of one day finding 'true' love alive.

Daniel's father, Rita had learnt all too soon, confused love with lust.

Throughout their 25 year marriage they had led almost separate lives, linked only by their address and, latterly, Daniel. She couldn't leave, she had nowhere to go. Besides, Daniel's dad loved him.

Her only ally, her sister-in-law Gloria, had been disowned by the family when she herself had fallen in love.

Rita didn't even know where Gloria lived any more. No one in the family spoke of her – was allowed to speak of her. Rita still missed Gloria. She had always said what she thought, followed her own instincts and refused to be bowed by the conventions around her. Falling in love and setting up home with her lover had been the final straw that tipped a very straight-laced family's sensitivities over the edge.

***

If Daniel had been allowed to ask his auntie what falling in love felt like, he would have got a very different answer from his mother's.

When Gloria first laid eyes on Frankie, across a crowded lecture hall, her heart seemed to stop beating. The world stopped turning on its axis and she'd had to grab the side of the lectern to prevent herself sinking to her knees.

58

Just about composing herself in order to deliver her lecture – 'The Influence of Gertrude Jekyll''s Planting Patterns on 20th Century Gardens' – Gloria had found it hard to stop looking at the beautiful student five rows back.

Was she imagining it? Or was the student also avidly watching her every move?

Gloria felt hot and cold at the same time, her mouth went dry and she found it hard to concentrate on her notes. By the end of the lecture she was shaking, she had to remember to breathe. Frankie had bounded up on to the stage immediately after the lecture, proffering a glass of water and, as Gloria would repeat for years after: 'You had me at hello...'

For two years the pair spent an awful lot of time together, talking horticulture, but the relationship of student and lecturer forbade anything more.

On the day Frankie graduated with a degree in Horticulture and Garden Design – first class honours – Gloria took her former student out for dinner to celebrate.

As if by some unspoken agreement drawn up in a previous life, they went back to Gloria's house, and Frankie never left.

When their respective families found out that Gloria had moved in one of her former students, the scandal was just too much.

The couple were ostracised by their families.

They both regretted the situation, but bound by their love for each other they had no choice.

Gloria particularly regretted the loss of her sister-in-law, Rita. She knew only too well what her brother was like, and she'd always got on really well with Rita. What a life she must have.

Hearing about the birth of Daniel had made her so happy for Rita, but she lamented the loss of a nephew. All attempts to get back in touch had been thwarted by both her brother and her parents.

But she couldn't give up Frankie. Frankie was the very air she breathed, her inspiration, her *'raison d'être'*. Without Frankie her life would be truly empty.

From the moment they met, the world had changed. Everything was brighter, fresher, more vibrant.

Every single lyric of every single love song she had ever heard actually meant something. She had never felt anything quite like it. Never dared to hope that she – anyone – could have found something quite so powerful, so complete, so utterly glorious.

Every cliché ever uttered made sense, particularly the one about being a teenager again. Gloria was twenty years older than Frankie.

But love had conquered everything.

Any doubts which had fleetingly crossed Gloria's mind – and they had been few and trivial - were swept away by a tide of emotion stronger than she had ever experienced.

It felt right, and she had known it was meant.

And it still felt so comfortable and warm – like sinking into a hot bath and letting the scented water caress every part of her body.

For more than 20 years they had shared everything. As Gloria sat sipping a cup of Earl Grey in the renovated Victorian conservatory which overlooked their beloved garden, she saw Frankie, languidly dead heading a stunning white rose bush. The bush had been a gift from Frankie to Gloria on their 10th anniversary. The garden they had created together was full of anniversary gifts. The pair had had many anniversaries as they had shared so many "firsts" – and seconds and fifths and everythings.

Their relationship had grown alongside the garden, and, like a badly written romance novel, Gloria looked towards her lover as she walked up the garden path and her heart missed a beat. Her eyes sparkled and her whole body radiated joy.

The two women smiled at each other, embraced and, as Gloria wordlessly poured more tea, they sat and talked until the sun went down.

Maybe one day, thought Gloria as she later stroked her partner's naked shoulder, she'd be able to meet Daniel.

What questions she could answer for him.

Birch Twigs and Velvet Ice-cream
Elizabeth Ducie

Bang!

"Oh my God, what's that?" I shoot upright and peer into the dark night. Not gunfire - too loud. Could it be a bomb? "What's happened? What was that noise? Why've we stopped? Let's get out of here."

Oleg applies the brake and kills the engine. I'm in complete darkness on a deserted road in a rattle-trap car some idiot has just tried to blow up. I can't see my watch, but I know it's getting on for two in the morning.

I feel a blast of freezing air as Oleg opens the door and heaves his bulk out. His heavy footsteps tramp round the front of the car and then silence. Motionless, I try to catch the slightest sound. Suppose there's a terrorist out there. He could kill Oleg, then come for me.

The car door opens and Oleg eases himself back in. "Tyre go bang. We wait help."

"The tyre?" I could weep with relief. Changing a tyre is no problem. I've done it myself more than once.

"Come on then, get the spare out and I'll help."

"No spare. Went bang yesterday."

I'm silenced. We haven't seen another car since we left the airport.

"Help not long. An hour. Maybe two."

I shiver. I'll be a frozen corpse by then. No, this needs more rapid action. I grab my mobile. Good thing I've memorised my interpreter's number. I dial carefully and grin at Oleg when Sveta answers.

"Da?"

"Sveta – thank god – we need help ..." Words tumble over themselves as I try to explain.

"OK, stop. Give the phone to Oleg".

Oleg talks rapidly in Russian before handing back my mobile. Sveta is still on the line.

"I'm not far away. Stay in the car – I'll be there soon".

I pull my coat tightly around me and wait, peering out every few seconds at the empty road.

What possessed me to come to Russia? I've regretted it ever since I landed at that awful airport with its missing light bulbs and long, shuffling queues. Once I get back home, I'll never roam again.

I'd been so happy when I'd got this job. All my friends were really envious. The advertisement had talked about excitement, responsibility and travel. After six months, my record had been an uncomfortable few days in down-town Amman, a couple of quick trips to Scandinavia, and several weeks in Brussels. Hardly the jet-setting life. I'd finally tackled my boss about it.

"Stan, you promised me I'd get my own accounts within a few months. All I'm doing is picking up the bits Mark Jenkins doesn't want."

Stan had smiled at me.

"As it happens, I want to talk to you about that. How do you fancy three months in Moscow? Head Office wanted to send Jenkins, he's been there before. But I persuaded them to give you a try.

I'd jumped at it. I'd always wanted to visit Russia. I hadn't thought twice about why Mark seemed happy I'd beaten him to the assignment. Now I was beginning to understand.

It's not the weather. I was prepared for that, even in January. Admittedly, it was a shock that the snow is only white for a day or so. I hadn't realised it would turn so quickly into piles of brown sludge, coating boots, floors and cars. Nor is it the Cyrillic alphabet. I've learned that quite quickly. It isn't even the food, although I'm pretty sick of cabbage already.

My real problem is the people. Girls serving in shops bark "what?" when I'm standing waiting to be served. That's when they're being helpful. The rest of the time, they just ignore me. Waitresses, impatient with my stumbling attempts at Russian, slap my plate in front of me disdainfully. When I try to say "good morning" to people I meet in my apartment block, all I get is a grunt – or total silence. In three weeks, I haven't had a proper conversation with anyone.

Now I'm stuck in a broken-down Volga in the middle of nowhere, having just taken a three hour flight from Moscow.

"Look, lady" Suddenly Oleg points into the distance. I see a faint glow which quickly becomes two sweeping beams of light. As the car pulls up beside us, I throw open my door, jump out and run, slipping and sliding, towards the comforting figure of my interpreter.

"I thought it was a bomb, a gun, someone trying to kill us, then I thought we'd freeze – I'm so glad to see you." My words fall over themselves as relief floods through me.

Sveta gives me a big hug and helps me into the front of the second vehicle. She has a few words with Oleg, then climbs in beside me.

"You need warming up – I have an idea." She will tell me no more and we drive through the darkness for ten minutes or so. Sveta makes a couple of calls on her mobile. I check my watch – nearly two thirty. I wonder if I will see my hotel room any time soon.

When the car stops, I'm surprised to see a small wooden hut in a clearing, surrounded by birch trees. Strings of fairy lights hang from the branches. The snow crunches under my feet. As we push our way through the double doors into the hut, the temperature rises dramatically.

We're met by Lydia, the owner of the company I'd come to visit. I've met her before and expected to see her tomorrow morning (or rather, later this morning) for meetings. She's always seemed brisk and business-like. Now she's off-duty and relaxed. A middle-aged women who obviously likes her food, her swimsuit does nothing to hide a generous girth, but she is completely unselfconscious.

"Welcome to my sauna" she says, throwing her arms as wide as her smile. Her English fails her at this point and she continues in a stream of Russian as she gestures me to take off my coat and boots. She hands me a huge sheet and a couple of fluffy bath towels, before disappearing into the inner part of the hut. Sveta turns her back on me and starts stripping off.

"Next time, you bring a swimsuit" says Sveta "but this time, just wrap the sheet round you." Quickly pulling off my clothes and winding the huge piece of cotton around myself, I follow Sveta into the sauna, gasping as a cloud of damp hot air envelops me.

65

"You should stay on the bottom bench until you get used to the heat, " says Sveta, climbing to the top level "it's cooler there". Gingerly lowering myself onto a towel, I realise cool is a relative term.

The room is tiny, barely big enough for three of us, and made completely of wood. Benches at three different heights line the back wall. In the corner is the box of coals from which the fierce heat rises. All around this, the wood is blackened, as though numerous fires have tried, but just failed, to break out.

Lydia grabs a bunch of twigs from a bowl of water and shakes them over the hot coals which sizzle and spit. Sweet-smelling steam clouds my vision. Sweat rolls down my body and I struggle to breathe. Lydia beats her arms and legs with the twigs and gives me a questioning look.

"Go on, try it" coaxes Sveta "it feels wonderful." Unable to think of any reason to refuse, I shrug and lie on my face. Lydia loosens the sheet and removes my slippers. There is something quite sensual about being undressed in this way by a near stranger in raging heat. The next minute the twigs are flicked across my back, at first gently, then harder. It's not painful. In fact the leaves feel like feathers stroking my skin. But the air is stirred around my body. Fiery waves swirl around me, burning their way into my mouth and nose. I close my eyes and hold my breath.

Just when I can stand it no longer, Lydia drops the twigs and heads for the door. Sveta jumps down from her perch and grabs my hand.

"Come on, time to cool off".

Bundling my sheet around me, I follow the two women through the hut in confusion. Have I missed another part of the building, maybe a shower room? To my amazement, they head straight for the front door and throw themselves into the snow. They roll around, squealing with laughter.

Without stopping to think, I plunge down a small bank and throw myself backwards. The feel of cold snow on my burning body is like velvet ice cream, soothing rather than painful. I rub handfuls along my arms and legs, enjoying the stinging sensation. Then I lie still, gazing upwards. The earlier clouds have gone. Brilliant stars are scattered across the black sky and the moon is full.

Sveta's voice breaks my reverie "Back inside – you'll get too cold." Retrieving my sheet from the snow, I head back to the hut, teeth chattering.

We rush back into the sauna to stop the shivers. Over the next couple of hours, we repeat the pattern two or three times. At some point, Lydia and Sveta both lose their damp swimsuits and I stop worrying about the sheet slipping. I learn to massage the others using the birch twigs and even venture onto the highest bench for a few minutes.

Finally, we return to the main room and wrap ourselves in bath towels. We pull on thick knitted socks and sit around the stove, waiting for supper (or should that be breakfast?) to be served. Drinking beer and eating fried shrimp, I realise I am laughing and joking with these two new friends and understand what Lydia is saying, even without an interpreter.

Maybe it was my new friend with the birch twigs. Or the magic of crisp white snow on bare skin. Maybe I just needed to look at life and the people of Russia in a different way. Looking out of the window, I see the darkness starting to lighten with the dawn. This is one January morning I'm unlikely to forget. Perhaps I won't book that return ticket just yet.